CIVIL RIGHTS STORIES

Racial Equality

Written by Anita Ganeri with illustrations by Toby Newsome

FRANKLIN WATTS

LONDON • SYDNEY

Foreword by Arike Oke

My mum is white-British and my dad is Yoruba-Nigerian (or Black-West African). When I was little I was called 'half-caste', referring to a word that came from an idea of levels of racial purity. Now I self-identify as 'mixed-race' and Black, until better words come along.

Better words will come, and they will come because books like this help us to grow, and learn more about why we do what we do, why we think the way we think, and how inequalities can be defeated over time. We work together to make change. Nelson Mandela was backed by people all around the world to help him bring down the apartheid system in South Africa. Black Lives Matter is strong as a movement, because we stand together in it.

This book will help parents and carers of children begin to explore the topic of racial equality together. As a child, I knew of and could sense the unfairness of the anger directed at both of my parents for their relationship and their family, but I couldn't understand where it came from. For children, this book is the beginning of understanding.

Arike Oke
Managing Director for Black Cultural Archives

Arike Oke is the Managing Director for Black Cultural Archives, the home of Black British history. She's worked in heritage for over 15 years, from the seminal Connecting Histories project in Birmingham, to building Wellcome Collection's archive, and co-convening Hull's first official Black History Month. Formerly Co-Chair of the Association of Performing Arts Collections, she advises the National Archives, BAFTA and the UK government's Home Office, is a Group Board member at Notting Hill Genesis, and is a fellow of the Arts Council's Museums and Resilient Leadership programme.

CONTENTS

WHAT IS RACIAL EQUALITY?

Everyone has the right to be equal. It doesn't matter what you look like or where you come from. You have the right to be treated in the same way as everybody else.

Racial equality is when everyone is treated the same, regardless of their race or skin colour. Unfortunately, there are people who believe that they are better than others and treat them badly or unfairly. When this happens because of a person's race or the colour of their skin, it is called racism.

In many countries today, racism is banned by law. It is against the law to insult, harm or discriminate against a person because of their race or skin colour.

Many people around the world campaigned for years to get these laws, often putting their own lives at risk.

Sometimes, these laws are broken or ignored. Not everyone gets the racial equality they deserve. There have been many breakthroughs, but there is still racism today.

SKIN COLOUR AND PREJUDICE

Since ancient times, false ideas about skin colour have influenced how people are treated. People with lighter skin were believed to be more powerful, more important and more beautiful than those with darker skin. This white privilege is still in place today.

As white people began to trade with Africa and Asia in the 14th century, they bought and sold servants and slaves from the countries they visited. Slaves with darker brown skin were often treated worse than those with lighter brown skin.

Much later, from the 1750s, Britain controlled large parts of India. From the 1880s, European nations colonised (took over) parts of Africa (see pages 12–13). The Europeans stereotyped people of colour. Black and brown skin became a sign that someone was poor, uneducated, dirty, stupid or dangerous. White skin became a sign of being rich, educated, clean, clever and pure.

Racist people still believe in some or all of these stereotypes today. Overcoming this prejudice is a key aim in the fight for racial equality.

A HOSTILE TAKEOVER

From the 15th century, white European settlers began arriving in North America. Almost from the start, they were hostile to the Native Americans – the people who had lived there for thousands of years. For Native Americans, the results were disastrous.

Millions of Native Americans were killed by diseases brought by the settlers, such as measles and smallpox, to which they had no immunity. Later, fierce battles were fought as Europeans tried to seize indigenous land. Armed with traditional weapons, Native Americans stood little chance against the Europeans' guns.

Europeans saw the Native Americans as 'wild' and 'savages', who did not deserve equal rights. In 1830, US President, Andrew Jackson, passed the Indian Removal Act. This law allowed the government to seize Native American lands and force people to move onto reservations that had poor soil, little water and terrible weather.

The Native American struggle against racism continues. The 1968 Indian Bill of Rights – and later, the American Indian Religious Freedom Act of 1978 – brought some important breakthroughs, but not the right to own the land they live on. This means that, even today, many Native Americans struggle to escape the poverty of the reservations or get a decent education.

THE ATLANTIC SLAVE TRADE

In the 18th century, millions of Black Africans were captured by European slave traders. They were marched to the coast in chains, then shipped from Africa to the USA, West Indies and Brazil.

The journey across the Atlantic Ocean could take months. The ships were badly overcrowded. Many slaves died of illness, starvation or were badly beaten. Sick slaves were sometimes thrown overboard, along with the dead.

On arrival, slaves were sold at auction as if they were objects, not human beings. Then, they were made to work on plantations, growing crops such as sugar and cotton.

Slaves made their owners very rich, but their own lives were miserable. They had no rights, even giving up their African names and taking their owners' names instead. They lived in terrible conditions and many died young because of overwork. If they tried to run away, they were beaten, branded or even murdered by their owners.

In 1807, the slave trade was banned in parts of the British Empire, including Australia and South Africa. Slavery itself was abolished in 1833. The Netherlands abolished slavery in 1863 and the USA in 1865, although freed slaves still faced many challenges.

THE 'SCRAMBLE FOR AFRICA'

After the Atlantic Slave Trade was banned, white Europeans were still drawn to Africa for its gold, timber, rubber and other riches. From the 1880s, countries including France, Britain and Belgium took control of much of the continent. They raced to claim as much land as they could. They divided Africa between them. In some places, people from the same tribe were left stranded on different sides of new national boundaries.

At that time, most white Europeans thought they were better than Black people. All over Africa, missions were set up to convert Africans to Christianity, the Europeans' religion.

White Europeans also forced Africans (and many Indian people who were made to go to Africa) to work very hard, harvesting crops and building roads and railroads. Those that rebelled or tried to resist were treated with violence and cruelty. Many were brutally murdered. The way Black and Asian people were thought of and treated at this time, compared with white people, is a part of why racism still exists today.

AUSTRALIA'S STOLEN LANDS

Mainland Australia's first people, the Aboriginal Peoples, have lived on the continent for more than 50,000 years. They are thought to have sailed from Asia, bringing their own culture and languages. For years, they have lived closely with the land, which they believe to be sacred.

Around 250 years ago, white British settlers came to Australia. They stole Aboriginal land, and spread diseases that killed thousands of Aboriginal Peoples. Thousands more were murdered. In just 100 years, the numbers of Aboriginal Peoples fell from around one million to 60,000.

Laws were passed that gave settlers the right to take over Aboriginal land. The laws said, falsely, that the land had been 'empty', and so had belonged to no one.

Racist laws against Aboriginal Peoples lasted well into the 20th century. Between 1910–1970, the Australian government took thousands of Aboriginal children, by force, from their homes, and sent them to live with white families.

The children were not allowed to speak their own languages, and often had to change their names.

Racism against Aboriginal Peoples continues in Australia today.

BRITAIN BY BOAT

On 22 June 1948, the HMT *Empire Windrush* sailed into Tilbury Docks, in Essex, England. On board were around 500 Black, British Commonwealth citizens from the West Indies.

After the Second World War (1939–45), Britain did not have enough people to work in hospitals, and on buses and trains. Many *Windrush* passengers had answered an advert to come and work in Britain. Later, many more people arrived from the West Indies, and from India and Pakistan.

HMT EMPIRE WINDRUSH

Far from being welcomed, the new arrivals were often called racist names and attacked. Many white landlords refused to rent rooms to Black and Asian people.

As more immigrants arrived, gangs of white racists took to the streets. In 1959, a Black man called Kelso Cochrane was stabbed to death by a white gang. His killers were never caught.

Kelso Cochrane

Over the years, Windrush immigrants have made a huge contribution to Britain. Despite this, racial inequality means that they have not always been treated well.

In 2018, the British government began deporting some of the Windrush people, and their families. The government accused them (wrongly) of not having documents to prove that they were allowed to live in the UK.

SEGREGATION IN THE USA

By the middle of the 20th century, Black people in the USA were still treated as second-class citizens. In many states, strict laws kept them apart from white people in places including schools and restaurants, and on public transport. This is known as segregation.

COLORED ENTRANCE

On 1 December 1955, in Montgomery, Alabama, a Black woman named Rosa Parks refused to give up her seat on the bus for a white person. She was arrested and ordered to pay a fine. In protest, pastor and Black civil rights leader, Martin Luther King Jr. called for a boycott of the city's buses. The boycott was planned for one day only – Monday 5 December. It would take courage for Black people to see it through.

Rosa Parks

Martin Luther King, Jr.

The bus boycott was a huge success and ended up lasting for over a year. Finally, on 20 December 1956, the order came from the US Supreme Court to end bus segregation. The next day, Martin Luther King Jr. and other leaders rode on the city's first integrated bus.

THE POWER OF WORDS

After the Montgomery bus boycott, Martin Luther King Jr. continued the struggle for racial equality in the USA. He travelled around the country, giving speeches, leading protest marches and joining student sit-ins.

On 28 August 1963, some 250,000 people – Black and white – marched through the US capital, Washington D.C. They stopped in front of the Lincoln Memorial to listen to speeches from the civil rights leaders.

Last to speak was Martin Luther King Jr. He talked about freedom and equal rights. In his famous "I Have a Dream ..." speech, he spoke about his hope that in the future people would not face prejudice based on the colour of their skin.

The following year, the US Congress passed the Civil Rights Bill.

In April 1968, Martin Luther King Jr. arrived in Memphis, Tennessee, to march with the city's refuse workers to demand better pay and working conditions. On the evening of 4 April, he was shot on his motel balcony and died later in hospital. His killer, a white man, called James Earl Ray, was a known racist.

In August 2011, The Martin Luther King, Jr. Memorial was completed to honour his work and legacy. This stone sculpture stands close to the Lincoln Memorial at 1964 Independence Avenue.

APARTHEID IN SOUTH AFRICA

From 1948–1991, South Africa came under apartheid rule. Apartheid means 'apartness' in Afrikaans (a language that is spoken in South Africa). Laws forced Black people and white people to live and work apart.

Black South Africans weren't allowed to vote in elections, had to live in poor housing in run-down townships and needed special passes to visit 'white' areas. Black and white people couldn't marry each other. Black people who broke these laws were beaten or sent to jail.

In 1962, Nelson Mandela, a leader of the African National Congress (ANC), was arrested and sentenced to life imprisonment. In June 1976, thousands of students in Soweto, a Black township, protested against apartheid. Things turned violent and the police opened fire. More than 175 people were killed and thousands more injured.

In 1990, after 27 years in prison, Mandela was released. He began talks with South Africa's white government to end apartheid. Four years later, elections were held in which all people of colour were able to vote for the first time. The ANC won the election, and Mandela became South Africa's first Black president.

Nelson Mandela

CULTURE AND PREJUDICE

People of colour have made huge contributions to culture, creating film, books, music, art, dance, television and theatre. Yet, Black artists are still linked mainly to music, such as rap, or to violent roles, such as gangsters in films. There are far fewer opportunities for people of colour to be represented in other areas, such as classical music, fine art or ballet.

In recent years, the film world has been criticised for not having more people of colour directing or in leading roles, nor rewarding Black actors for their work. In 2015 and 2016, no people of colour were nominated for acting awards at the Oscars in the USA. In 2020, only one Black actor received an acting nomination.

There are now campaigns for greater diversity, and there have been some breakthroughs. In 2016, actor Chadwick Boseman – who sadly died in 2020 – starred as the superhero, King T'Challa, in the blockbusting *Black Panther* film.

Boseman broke many stereotypes. He became one of very few Black leading actors who was given a leading Hollywood role. He gave Black people a Black superhero that they could identify with.

Chadwick Boseman

BLACK LIVES MATTER

Black Lives Matter is a US civil rights movement. It was set up in 2013 by three Black women – Opal Tometi, Patrisse Cullors and Alicia Garza.

Black Lives Matter was a response to the fatal shooting of Black teenager, Trayvon Martin, by George Zimmerman, who has white-German and Peruvian heritage. Prosecutors tried to show that this was a hate crime because Trayvon was Black, but Zimmerman was later found not guilty of murder or manslaughter.

Since 2013, Black Lives Matter protests and events have spread around the world to challenge racism and empower Black people.

Trayvon Martin

Opal Tometi

Patrisse Cullors

Alicia Garza

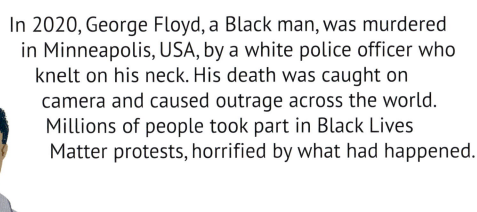

In 2020, George Floyd, a Black man, was murdered in Minneapolis, USA, by a white police officer who knelt on his neck. His death was caught on camera and caused outrage across the world. Millions of people took part in Black Lives Matter protests, horrified by what had happened.

Black Lives Matter is so important because it shows that we do not yet have racial equality. Until we do, then we cannot say that all lives matter.

Hopefully, movements like Black Lives Matter will mark the beginning of real and lasting change in the struggle for racial justice and equality.

RACIAL EQUALITY TODAY

For years, people have campaigned hard for racial equality. Today, in the 21st century, there are laws giving everyone equal rights, regardless of skin colour or race. Progress has been made, but laws and rights are sometimes ignored. Today, people of colour are still facing discrimination and violence.

Racism means that Black, Asian and other people of colour are more likely to be stopped and searched by the police. Discrimination causes many Black children to be labelled as troublemakers at school. Racism means that if you have an 'ethnic-sounding' name, you may be less likely to be offered a job.

Often white people refuse to see that they may be racist or are acting in a racist way. Because they are not affected by racism, some white people don't think carefully about their words and actions. They cause hurt and offence through ignorance. This is part of the problem and is a part of what is called white privilege.

Racism isn't a 'Black problem' that is fixed by, for example, electing a Black person as US president. Racism is a problem that can only be solved by the majority of people working towards a common goal and actively being anti-racist.

RACIAL EQUALITY TIMELINE

Here is a list of moments in history found in this book that help to tell the story of the ongoing fight for racial equality.

1300s: Europeans trading with Asia and Africa buy and sell slaves along trade routes.

1400s: White settlers arrive in North America, causing the deaths of millions of Native Americans.

1700s: The Atlantic Slave Trade begins. Millions of Black African men, women and children are captured and forced into slavery. Many die or are murdered on the slave ships that transport them across the Atlantic.

1780s: White settlers begin to arrive in Australia. They steal land from the Aboriginal Peoples, spread diseases and kill thousands.

1807: The slave trade is banned in parts of the British Empire.

1830: The Indian Removal act forces Native Americans off their lands and on to reservations.

1833: The British Empire abolishes slavery.

1863: The Netherlands abolishes slavery.

1865: The USA abolishes slavery.

1877: The US introduces strict segregation laws (also known as the Jim Crow laws) for Black people.

1880s: Belgium, Britain, France, Germany, Italy, Portugal and Spain exploit Africa's people and rich resources during the 'Scramble for Africa'.

1910–1970s: Thousands of Aboriginal children are stolen from their families.

1948: HMT *Empire Windrush* brings the first wave of immigrants to Britain from the Commonwealth. New arrivals are treated with hostility.

1948–91: South Africa comes under apartheid rule.

1955: Rosa Parks is arrested for refusing to give up her seat on a bus. It becomes an important moment in the fight for Black civil rights.

1962: Nelson Mandela is imprisoned.

1963: Martin Luther King Jr. leads many protest marches and makes many speeches, including his famous *I Have a Dream* … speech on the Lincoln Memorial, in Washington DC.

1964: US congress passes the Civil Rights Bill.

1968: Martin Luther King Jr is assassinated.

1968: In the US, the Indian Bill of Rights is passed.

1976: Over 175 people are killed in the Soweto uprising, protesting over apartheid.

1978: In the US the American Indian Religious Freedom Act is passed. Native Americans are still denied the rights to own the land they live on.

1990: Nelson Mandela is released.

1994: Nelson Mandela becomes South Africa's first Black president.

2008: Barack Obama becomes the first Black president of the USA.

2011: The Martin Luther King Jr. Memorial sculpture is completed in Washington D.C.

2013: Black Lives Matter is set up in response to the shooting of Black teenager Trayvon Martin.

2018: The British government begins illegally deporting Windrush generation families.

2020: George Floyd is murdered by a police officer kneeling on his neck. This sparks outrage and Black Lives Matter protests across the world.

GLOSSARY

abolish to formally end (in law)

boycott to refuse to buy or use something

branded to be permanently marked with a branding iron

civil rights the rights to equality and to political and social freedom

colonise to settle in a land and then control its people

Commonwealth a group of countries (many which were part of the former British Empire); the Commonwealth of Nations

discriminate to treat people differently based on prejudice

empower to give someone the confidence or the power to do something

hate crime a crime motivated by prejudice based on, for example, someone's race or sex

hostile aggressive and unfriendly

ignorance a lack of knowledge

immigrant a person who goes to live in a foreign country

immunity protection from a deadly disease

indigenous the people who are native to a particular place

landlord someone who owns or rents out land or buildings

measles an infectious disease that causes fever and a rash, and can cause death

mission Christians who are spreading the Christian religion; the buildings from which they spread their faith

plantation an estate where crops are grown

poverty the state of being extremely poor

prejudice dislike or hostility toward someone that is based on false ideas about that person

rebel to resist authority; to take action to oppose something

refuse worker someone who's job is to take away rubbish from the streets

reservation an area of land set aside for a group of indigenous people, such as Native Americans

settler someone who moves to live in a new place along with others from the same group

smallpox an infectious disease that causes fever and skin lesions, and can cause death

stereotype widely believed and often simplistic idea of a type of person

township a city (or part of a city) that is officially for (mainly) Black residents

white privilege the advantages that white people have because they are not subject to racism in a society that discriminates against Black people and other people of colour.

BOOKS TO READ

Children in Our World: Racism and Intolerance
by Louise Spilsbury and illustrated by Hanane Kai
(Wayland, 2018)

Children in Our World: Rights and Equality
by Marie Murray and illustrated by Hanane Kai
(Wayland, 2021)

Questions and Feelings About: Racism
by Anita Ganeri and illustrated by Ximena Jeria
(Franklin Watts, 2020)

Info Buzz: Black History (series)
by various authors,
(Franklin Watts, 2019)

INDEX

Franklin Watts
First published in Great Britain in 2021 by The Watts Publishing Group
Copyright © The Watts Publishing Group, 2021

All rights reserved.

HB ISBN: 978 1 4451 7139 5
PB ISBN: 978 1 4451 7140 1

Printed and bound in Dubai

Editor: Amy Pimperton
Designer: Peter Scoulding
Cover design: Peter Scoulding
Illustrations: Toby Newsome

Page 2 photograph
© Adenike Oke

FSC
www.fsc.org
MIX
Paper from responsible sources
FSC® C104740

Franklin Watts, an imprint of
Hachette Children's Group
Carmelite House
50 Victoria Embankment
London EC4Y 0DZ

An Hachette UK Company
www.hachette.co.uk
www.franklinwatts.co.uk

All facts and statistics were correct
at the time of printing.